Gemstone Dragons

EMERALD'S BLOOMING SECRET

The Gemstone Dragons series

Opal's Time to Shine

Ruby's Fiery Mishap

Topaz's Spooky Night

Emerald's Blooming Secret

Gemstone Dragons

EMERALD'S BLOOMING SECRET

Samantha M. Clark

ILLUSTRATED BY

Hollie Hibbert

BLOOMSBURY
CHILDREN'S BOOKS
NEW YORK LONDON OXFORD NEW DELHI SYDNEY

BLOOMSBURY CHILDREN'S BOOKS
Bloomsbury Publishing Inc., part of Bloomsbury Publishing Plc
1385 Broadway, New York, NY 10018

BLOOMSBURY, BLOOMSBURY CHILDREN'S BOOKS, and the Diana logo
are trademarks of Bloomsbury Publishing Plc

First published in the United States of America in December 2022
by Bloomsbury Children's Books

Bloomsbury books may be purchased for business or promotional use.
For information on bulk purchases please contact Macmillan Corporate and
Premium Sales Department at specialmarkets@macmillan.com

Library of Congress Cataloging-in-Publication Data
Names: Clark, Samantha M., author. | Hibbert, Hollie, illustrator.
Title: Emerald's blooming secret / by Samantha M. Clark ; illustrated by Hollie Hibbert.
Description: New York : Bloomsbury Children's Books, 2022. | Series: Gemstone dragons ;
book 4 | Audience: Ages 7-10. | Audience: Grades 2-3.
Summary: Emerald has collected every wildflower seed in Gemstone Valley so he can grow
a special garden for Sapphire's birthday, but when the other dragons and creatures notice no
flowers are blooming in the rest of the Valley, he tries to make things right.
Identifiers: LCCN 2022022251 (print) | LCCN 2022022252 (e-book)
ISBN 978-1-5476-1092-1 (paperback) • ISBN 978-1-5476-1093-8 (e-book)
Subjects: CYAC: Dragons—Fiction. | Sharing—Fiction. | Flowers—Fiction. | Fantasy. | LCGFT:
Fantasy fiction.
Classification: LCC PZ7.1.C579 Em 2022 (print) | LCC PZ7.1.C579 (e-book) | DDC [Fic]—dc23
LC record available at https://lccn.loc.gov/2022022251
LC e-book record available at https://lccn.loc.gov/2022022252

Book design by Jeanette Levy
Typeset by Westchester Publishing Services
Printed and bound in the U.S.A.
4 6 8 10 9 7 5

To find out more about our authors and books
visit www.bloomsbury.com and sign up for our newsletters.

For Penelope and Daisy,
who are as sweet as roses

EMERALD'S BLOOMING SECRET

chapter one

KEEPING SECRETS

Emerald raced out of Sparkle Cave. He was late! Amber had told all the Gemstone Dragons to go to the daisy patch near the Friendly Forest at nine o'clock for a secret meeting about Sapphire's birthday party. Sapphire was the oldest and wisest of all the Gemstone Dragons, and everyone wanted her party to be special. Emerald couldn't wait for the party. He was planning a surprise of his own, and he knew all the dragons would love it.

When he got close to the daisy patch, he skidded to a halt behind Aquamarine, who was looking out to make sure Sapphire didn't come this way. "Has the meeting started?" Emerald asked.

Aquamarine nodded. "Do you know what the dragon who was late to the meeting said?"

"No, what?"

"It was just a matter of time. Get it? Because you're late, you have a lack of time?" Aquamarine laughed.

"Har har," Emerald said. He didn't think the joke was all that funny. He hurried on to the meeting.

When he got to the cluster of dragons, Amber was asking everyone what they were going to bring to the party.

"I'll bake the cake," Diamond said, grinning. "Sapphire loves my cakes. She should have only the best."

"Okay, Diamond is doing the cake," Amber said, jotting it down in her notebook.

"We'll make the other food," said Topaz, pointing to herself and Ruby.

"Yeah," said Ruby, then added under her breath, "and it'll be just as yummy as the cake."

Emerald tried not to laugh. Diamond always thought what he did was the best.

"I thought we could make a special stage for the party," Obsidian said. "We could act out stories about Sapphire and even sing songs. Do you want to do that with me, Amber?"

"Sure! That's a great idea," Amber said. "What about decorations?"

Opal's paw shot up. "Aquamarine and I can do the decorations."

"Perfect," said Amber. "You're good at that. Your bedcave always looks wonderful."

Opal blushed. "Thank you, Amber. I'm not sure what we'll use to decorate, though. I'd love to decorate with flowers. Sapphire loves flowers! But I haven't seen many in Gemstone Valley."

"I noticed that too," said Garnet. "There are usually lots of flowers blooming around Sapphire's birthday, but not now."

A murmur went through the crowd

of dragons. Emerald could see that they were nodding and agreeing with Opal and Garnet. He stepped back, hoping no one would ask him about it.

"I need honeysuckle for my cake!" Diamond stomped his foot. "Sapphire likes it with lots of sweet honeysuckle."

"I'd love to have pansy petals for a salad," Topaz said.

"Mmmm, yes." Ruby rubbed her tummy thinking about it. "They taste so minty and they look so pretty."

Emerald shrank back even more.

"The stage would look great covered in flowers," said Obsidian. "Sapphire would love that too!"

Opal nodded. "She really would. But where are we going to find enough flowers?

Emerald?" She glanced around. Emerald had stepped so far back, he was no longer in the circle of dragons. "Where did Emerald go? He was just here."

Emerald wanted to hide so no one would ask him about the flowers. He thought about hurrying away, but it was too late. Amber spotted him.

"He's right there. Come and join us, Emerald."

He stepped forward again.

"Hey, Emerald," Opal said, "do you know what happened to all the flowers?"

"Uh, no." Emerald glanced down, trying to avoid the eyes of the other Gemstone Dragons. He felt as though they could see right into him and pluck out his secret. He didn't like keeping secrets, but if he told all the dragons what he was up to, it would ruin everything. He wanted them to be as surprised as Sapphire. He knew they were going to love it. "Maybe they're not growing because of the weather. I'll look into it."

Opal's face broke into a big smile. "Thank you, Emerald! If anyone can grow big beautiful flowers for Sapphire's birthday, it's you."

Emerald smiled back, but quickly

looked at the ground again. He didn't want his smile to give away just how close Opal was to the truth.

While Amber went over the birthday party plans, Emerald noticed something poking up from the ground right at his feet. A wildflower seed! He reached down and quickly pulled it into his paw before another dragon could see.

As soon as the meeting was over, Emerald hurried back to his bedcave. He shut the door tight, then went to the little box he'd hidden in a nook under his bedrock. Once he'd taken off the lid, he carefully placed the seed he had found inside.

Emerald sat back and stared at all the lovely seeds in the box. He had collected pretty much every wildflower seed in Gemstone Valley and was keeping them all safe in this box until the time was right. Tomorrow was Sapphire's birthday, and the more he thought about his plan, the more excited he got.

"I'm going to give you all my gemstone power," Emerald whispered to the seeds. "Then you are going to grow up so big and beautiful. You're going to make the best birthday present that Sapphire has ever had. I know it's going to be her favorite."

He smiled to himself as he imagined his great reveal. "All the dragons will love my gift. Everyone in Gemstone Valley will say how wonderful it is! Their eyes are going to light up. The dragons will ooh and aah and pat me on the back. They'll say I'm the best gift-maker ever. And it'll all be thanks to you. And me, of course."

Emerald chuckled. "Sleep well, little seeds. Tomorrow you will shine."

He closed the lid and put the box back into its hiding place.

He thought about the other dragons and how they wanted flowers for their gifts too. He thought about Opal wanting flowers for the party decorations. He felt a little guilty that he was keeping all the flowers for himself, but the other dragons would be fine. They always made wonderful presents for Sapphire. They were all so creative. Opal and Aquamarine would come up with other ideas for the party decorations.

For once, Emerald wanted his gift to be the most special. This time, it would be. He was sure of it.

He pushed his guilt down into the pit of his tummy, then smiled.

One more day. Then Sapphire and all the creatures in Gemstone Valley would really see what Emerald could create.

chapter two

PREPARATIONS MAKE PERFECT

* * * * * * * * * *

The next morning, Emerald woke up early. He wanted to be the first dragon outside so he could set up his surprise without anyone seeing.

GRRR.

Emerald's tummy rumbled loudly. "Not now, tummy. I don't have time to eat."

But he thought about how he might

mess up his gift if he was distracted by hunger. He couldn't have that!

"Okay, I'll quickly grab a snack in the kitchen. Then I'll start on my seeds."

Emerald dashed to the kitchen. No other dragons were in sight yet, which made him happy. He pulled a mango from the shelf, piled a yummy swirl of silicone on top, then gobbled it down. "Mmmm." He made another. Then another.

His tummy was feeling nice and full now, but maybe he could have just one more. He saw a big mango that looked extra juicy. He wanted it. He reached toward the mango, but then . . .

BANG!

The kitchen door slammed open and

Amber strolled in. "There you are, Emerald! I've been looking all over for you. But what are you doing here? You're not on breakfast duty."

"I wanted a snack," Emerald said, wishing he'd left earlier. "But I'm going now."

"Good, because we have to solve the flower problem." Amber tugged on Emerald's arm, leading him out of the kitchen.

"I really don't think it's going to be too much of a problem." Emerald looked anxiously down the hallway to his bedcave as Amber pulled him outside. He had to get his seeds ready and in position soon, or his present for Sapphire wouldn't grow in time.

"Look!" Amber motioned around them once they were outside Sparkle Cave. "There are fewer flowers than yesterday, and Opal and Aquamarine haven't picked any yet. Opal said they didn't want to disturb the plants, in the hope that they'd grow more flowers. But that hasn't happened. We have to do something."

Emerald blinked in the bright early morning sunlight, then stared at the grounds around the entrance to Sparkle Cave. Amber was right. There were trees, bushes, and grass, but no flowers in sight.

"It could be because of the soil," Amber said. "Use your gemstone power to make it better."

Emerald didn't want to waste his gemstone power now. He had plans for it.

He shook his head. "I don't think it's the soil. The bushes and grass are growing well."

Amber tapped a claw on her cheek. "Hmmm. That's true. They are very green. Do flowers need something different?"

"No, but they are seasonal. I think it's the weather." He cringed as soon as he said the words. The day was beautifully sunny, the perfect weather for flowers to bloom. But he had to say something to keep Amber from asking questions.

And he had to get back to his bedcave to set up the seeds. He didn't want to lose the sunlight either.

"I'm going to look into it more, Amber," Emerald said. "You leave it to me."

"Okay. But are you sure you don't need help? It's very important."

Emerald nodded. "I'll take care of everything."

As he raced back into Sparkle Cave, Emerald again felt that twinge of guilt pinching his tummy. But he was taking care of everything. Sapphire was going to get plenty of flowers for her birthday. They'd just be part of *his* present. It didn't matter how she got the flowers, as long as she got them, Emerald figured. And besides, he told himself, the other dragons were going to love the gift so much, they'd understand. He imagined them crowding around him saying "Wow" and "You're incredible" and "Your gift is amazing!" Everything was going to be perfect when they saw what he had planned. He just had to get it ready.

It was now later than he had wanted to start. More and more Gemstone Dragons were waking up and wandering around Shimmering Hall and the hallways to the bedcaves. Emerald had to hurry if he was going to keep his gift a secret. He had to get his seeds up to Mineral Mountain before any of the others went up there.

After closing his bedcave door tight, he carefully pulled out the box from its hiding place and lifted the lid.

"It's time, little seeds! Time for you to grow big and strong." He smiled down at his collection. It always amazed him how something so tiny and plain could grow into something as big and majestic as a flower or a tree. That was one of the reasons he loved his gemstone power. Having the ability to help things grow made him feel good. And now he was using his power in a way that would make Sapphire and all the other creatures in Gemstone Valley scream in delight. He couldn't wait to see their faces and know it was all because of him.

Staring at the box, Emerald concentrated on his gemstone and asked it to make the seeds strong. He wanted them to grow as big as possible, the biggest flowers any Gemstone Valley creature had ever seen. His green scales rippled and the emerald on his chest glowed bright. As he watched, the seeds in the box glowed, too, then they plumped up, filled with his power.

Emerald grinned. He was sure that Sapphire's present was going to be the Best Gift Ever.

chapter three

BEST LAID PLANS

Once he had put all his power into the seeds, Emerald tried to close the lid on the box. It was harder now that the seeds had grown bigger, but he managed to balance the lid enough to keep the seeds from spilling out. He would have to carry the box carefully.

He opened the door to his bedcave a tiny bit, then peered into the hallway. He didn't want anyone to see what he was doing, and there were more dragons around to avoid now.

Emerald wished again that he hadn't eaten that extra snack. Then he wouldn't have been found by Amber and delayed. He sighed. There was nothing he could do about it. He just had to stay away from other dragons until his plan was complete.

With the hallway clear, he stepped out from his bedcave and hurried for the entrance to Sparkle Cave. He couldn't run fast. He didn't want to trip and drop the seeds. That would ruin everything!

He rounded a corner. Almost there, he thought, and—

"Hey, Emerald!" Ruby said as she and

Topaz walked up to him. "What are you doing?"

"Nothing," Emerald said quickly. "I'm not doing anything. Why would I be doing anything?"

"I—" Ruby began, but Emerald interrupted her.

"No time! No time!" He pushed on. He could see the entrance. He was almost outside.

"Morning, Emerald," Obsidian said, coming out of Shimmering Hall. He stepped in front of Emerald, leaned close, then whispered, "I'm going to start building the stage. It'll look so wonderful with lots of flowers on it. I hope you can make them grow."

"Me too," Emerald mumbled, then

dashed out of Sparkle Cave before anyone else could stop him.

Lots more dragons and other magical creatures from Gemstone Valley were outside now. Opal and Aquamarine were playing with some unifoals. Diamond was showing off his wind power to some young gnomes. And Amber was peering under bushes—probably looking for flowers, Emerald thought.

Emerald had to stay away from them. He couldn't let his plan be discovered. He was sure the dragons would want some of the wildflower seeds for themselves. But for his gift to be truly spectacular, he needed to have them all.

He made a beeline to the spot on Mineral Mountain where he planned to sow the seeds. Done just right, the seeds would grow beautiful flowers in the shape of the words "WE LOVE SAPPHIRE" on the side of the mountain in lots of pretty colors. Creatures from all over Gemstone Valley would be able to see the words if he planted the seeds properly. He had to be precise about where each seed was placed, or else the letters wouldn't show up right and the effect would be ruined.

"Higher! Higher!" At the base of the mountain below Emerald, the young gnomes were shouting at Diamond as his wind power pushed a ball into the air.

Emerald gritted his teeth, wishing again that he had left earlier so there would be fewer distractions.

"Come on, Emerald," he murmured

to himself. "Get the seeds in place and everything will be great."

He took a deep breath. He wanted the gift to be perfect. He checked the location again, then dropped two seeds on the ground and smoothed earth over them with his back paw. He shuffled forward and dropped three seeds, smoothing the earth over them too. Another step forward, another few seeds, then another and another.

"It's going too high! STOP IT!" a young gnome shouted.

Emerald glanced in the direction of the shout. Diamond's wind had pushed the ball into a tree.

Emerald watched as the little gnomes

pointed sadly at the ball and Diamond shook his head. *Nothing for me to worry about. Diamond will get the ball back. He always figures out everything,* Emerald thought, stepping again to plant more seeds.

But his back paw hit a rock. He tripped, falling onto the ground. The box tumbled out of his arms, and seeds sprayed all around him.

"No!"

Emerald scrambled to collect them. As he searched for the seeds, he heard Diamond say, "I know, I'll make a tornado! That'll bring the ball down, and it'll look fun too."

Emerald's eyes grew wide as he watched

a small tornado whip up below him. It tossed the ball out of the tree, then headed up Mineral Mountain.

The tornado was headed right for him and his seeds!

"NO!" Emerald stood up and waved at Diamond. "Keep it away!"

"What?" Diamond shouted.

"Keep the wind away!" Emerald called back.

But he was too late. The tornado danced right over Emerald's path, and the seeds flew up from the ground.

Diamond finally stopped his gemstone power. The tornado twisted away, then died down, and Diamond came running over.

"Are you all right, Emerald?" he asked. "My tornado didn't hurt you, did it? It wasn't strong."

Emerald didn't answer. He was staring at the ground.

All the seeds were gone.

chapter four

A SCAVENGER HUNT

"What's wrong, Emerald?" Amber hurried over to him with a pile of twigs in her arms. "You look worried."

"He tripped," Diamond said. "My tornado couldn't have pushed him down. I would never make it that strong. I can control my pow— Hey, what are all those twigs for?"

"They're for the stage." Amber smiled broadly. "We've come up with a really fun design. It's going to look like a castle, and there will be a throne inside for Sapphire to sit on. It'll look great surrounded by flowers. Emerald, have you solved the problem with the flowers yet? Sapphire will be in the Friendly Forest all day, but we have to get everything ready before she gets back if we're going to make it a surprise."

But Emerald wasn't really listening to them. He was still staring at the ground. All his seeds were gone. His birthday present for Sapphire was ruined!

"You look very upset." Amber put a paw on Emerald's shoulder. "I'm sorry. I've been putting all this pressure on you, when the flowers probably just don't want to grow right now in this weather, like you said. You know them better than anyone."

Amber dropped her twigs and gave Emerald a hug. "I know you've tried to help. Don't worry about Sapphire's birthday party. Opal and Aquamarine will find other things to decorate with. It's going to be wonderful no matter what."

"I . . . oh, yeah, good," Emerald said, pretending that was exactly what was worrying him.

That twinge of guilt returned to his tummy. Amber was being so nice, and she didn't know that they had no flowers because he'd been keeping all the seeds for himself—or at least, for the Best Gift Ever that he had planned to give to Sapphire.

And now, the seeds were all gone and the dragons wouldn't see it.

Amber gave him a big smile. Then she and Diamond headed back down Mineral Mountain with the twigs.

Emerald frowned. He couldn't let his idea for the Best Gift Ever be a failure. He had to find the seeds. And he had to find them fast. He didn't want any of the other dragons getting them.

Emerald picked up his box and set off in search of the seeds. He spotted three on the ground near where he had fallen. He swiped them up quickly and put them in the box. A few more were under a

bush farther on. He gathered those too. He looked around and saw a bunch of seeds sprinkled at the base of a tree. He hurried over and snatched them up.

Hope began to flow through Emerald. Almost a third of the seeds were safely back in his box. If he could find the rest quickly, he could still get them in the ground with enough time for them to grow before the start of the party.

Emerald continued to look around, his head down, his eyes searching every inch of the ground. Every time he spotted a seed, he ran over to it and snapped it up.

Diamond's tornado had thrown the seeds far. Emerald had wandered all the way down to the unicorn rings in Gemstone Valley, and he was still finding them! The unifoals Canterlope and Honeydoo galloped over and asked him if he was playing a new type of game, but he said, "No time! No time!" and continued to search.

"I'll have all the seeds in the ground soon," he told himself. "The Best Gift Ever will still be great!"

Emerald had just reached down to pick up another seed when—

RRRRIIIPPP

He swung around and saw something bright green poke up out of the soil. It was thicker than anything he'd ever seen grow before. He ran over to examine it, and as he got closer, it started to move. It wriggled. It waggled. It stretched up tall.

It was a stalk!

The stalk kept growing, leaves stretching out in all directions. It looked like the plant was erupting from the earth.

At the top of the stalk, Emerald saw a bud unfurl within the leaves. His mouth dropped open as the bud expanded into a beautiful and huge yellow sunflower.

"No flower grows this fast," Emerald mumbled, and his eyes widened as he understood what had happened. "This is one of my seeds. My gemstone power made it grow!"

chapter five

SUPER SEEDS

"It worked!" Emerald exclaimed, jumping in joy. "My gemstone power worked. And it worked really well!"

Emerald loved all trees and bushes and flowers. He loved the way each one was different, with different shaped leaves, different colored petals, and different flowery scents. He loved how they reached for the sun and rustled in the wind. And he especially loved that when a plant was sick, he, Emerald, had the power to make it better.

When Emerald had first had the idea for Sapphire's present, he had thought he could use his gemstone power to make the seeds grow just a little, enough that they'd have flowers. But he'd never dreamed they'd grow this big. He had turned the regular flower seeds into super seeds. The stalk in front of him came up to his belly, and the flower was as big as his head!

"With flowers like this, Sapphire's present will be even better than the Best Gift Ever," Emerald said to himself. "It'll be the Even Better Best Gift Ever! I have to get this flower into the right spot before the other dragons see it. They're going to want to use it for cakes or decorations."

Emerald grabbed the stalk and pulled. It wouldn't budge! He pulled again, then again, but the plant still didn't move. The roots had grown so strong from Emerald's power that they were gripping the soil tightly.

"Come on," Emerald whispered, as he tugged harder. "I'll replant you. I promise."

But the stalk was being stubborn. It had made a home in this spot and it didn't want to leave. As Emerald pulled, the stalk grew even taller.

"Let go!" Emerald told the flower. "I need you on the side of Mineral Mountain. Not here."

As if answering him, the flower sprouted a new leaf and another flower bud. The petals sprang out so quickly, they slapped Emerald in the face.

"Stop growing!" Emerald said. "I know what to do."

He stepped back and connected to his gemstone, asking it to stop the flower's growing. But no power came out!

"Oh no!" he said. "Did I use up all my power on the seeds? I've used my power a lot before, but it's never stopped working. This is the first time I've asked it to stop growth, though. Hmmm."

He tried again, this time asking his gemstone to help the plant. His emerald glowed bright sending his power into the flower. But it only made the stalk grow taller.

Emerald's shoulders drooped. "My power only helps plants grow. It won't stop them. And now I've put even more power into this flower. I'm going to need something else to move this plant."

Obsidian could probably use his gemstone power of strength to get the plant out of the ground, but if Emerald asked him, he'd have to explain where it had come from, and that would ruin the surprise. He had to keep this a secret.

"I know!" Emerald said. "I'll dig you out." Splaying his claws, he dug away at the soil around the flower's roots.

Finally the soil gave way and the roots lifted out. Emerald breathed a sigh of relief.

"Now I just have to get you up to the side of Mineral Mountain before the roots dry out. And without anyone seeing."

Luckily, the plant's stalk was bendy, so Emerald hid the box of seeds behind a rock, then bundled up the plant as best he could. Tucking the flowers under his arm, he made his way to the spot on the mountain where he had started to make his gift, smiling at how happy all the dragons were going to be if he succeeded.

chapter six

ANOTHER HITCH IN THE PLAN

Excitement bloomed inside Emerald. His plan was finally getting back on track. Once this plant was in place, he'd come back for his box and find the other seeds. He could still make the Best Gift Ever.

The only problem was, the plant wasn't easy to carry. To keep it healthy on the journey, Emerald had to hold onto the soil around its roots. But little pieces of soil kept dropping onto the ground like crumbs from a copper chip cookie. He needed something to contain it.

"I know," he mumbled to himself. "I'll get a bowl from the kitchen."

He was close to Sparkle Cave now, so he set the plant down beside a bush, hiding the flowers underneath the bush's broad leaves.

"There. If any creature sees you, they'll think you're just part of the bush. I'll be right back."

Emerald hurried into Sparkle Cave and headed to the kitchen. His heart felt like it was pounding through his chest. This plan had not gone at all the way he wanted, but with any luck, he could still make Sapphire's Best Gift Ever. And now it would be even better!

In the kitchen, Emerald grabbed a large round mixing bowl with high sides. "Perfect," he whispered, then turned and bumped right into Diamond.

"Hey, what are you doing in here? I'm making the cake," Diamond said, frowning. "Where are the flowers? I'm still waiting for my honeysuckle."

Emerald tried to think of an excuse for why he needed a bowl if he wasn't making food. "I'm doing an experiment with some soil. I don't know if it'll work, though, so it might be good if you make the cakes without the honeysuckle. Good luck!" Emerald raced away from the kitchen.

Outside, Emerald rushed back to the

flower's hiding place, trying not to be seen by Amber and the other dragons, who were doing party preparations nearby.

"That was close," he whispered as he got back to the flower. "I can't get caught yet."

The bowl was the perfect size. Carefully, Emerald placed the plant's roots and the soil around them inside. "Much better. You're protected. Now let's get you up the mountainside."

Emerald smiled to himself. Soon he'd have one flower in place. Then he could plant the other seeds he'd found so far, and go look for more. The flowers would grow at different rates, but that would be okay. His gemstone power had made them so big, the words would be seen for miles.

He picked up the bowl with the plant and turned toward Mineral Mountain.

"Ahh!" Amber pointed at Emerald. "It's a flower! You are brilliant, Emerald. That flower is so big!"

Emerald glanced down. He'd forgotten to hide the flowers under his arm! The large sunflowers were gazing up toward the sun, like they were giving Amber a big old grin.

Amber ran over. "It's perfect, Emerald. Can you grow more?"

"Umm." Emerald thought about the seeds in his seed box. He was going to grow lots more flowers, but he couldn't tell Amber yet. It would ruin the big surprise! He had to think of something else. "It's fake," he blurted out.

Amber frowned. "Fake?"

Emerald nodded. "I made it . . . out of . . . special paper." He had to think about it as he said it.

"Wow," Amber said, touching one of the petals. "It feels so real."

Emerald pulled it away. "I don't have much of the special paper, but Opal and Aquamarine can use this one. I'm taking it to them now."

As he carried the bowl with the plant over to where Opal and Aquamarine were talking, Emerald felt like kicking himself. He hadn't been careful, and now he was going to have to give up one of his flowers. He also didn't like lying to the other dragons. But he couldn't tell them the truth yet. He thought about how proud of him they were going to be. It would be worth it when they saw how wonderful the Best Gift Ever was.

"Look what Emerald made," Amber said to Opal and Aquamarine. "He can only make this one flower for now, but you can do something with it, right?"

Opal nodded. "One is better than none. It's beautiful, Emerald. Thank you!"

Emerald felt that twinge of guilt again,

but he pushed it way, way down in his belly.

Aquamarine said, "What did the big flower say to the little flower? You're really growing, bud! Get it? Because flowers have buds." He laughed, making Amber and Opal chuckle too.

But Emerald didn't laugh. He had to get up to Mineral Mountain and get the seeds planted. He was running out of time!

"Enjoy," he said to them, then dashed to the unicorn rings, where he'd left the box of seeds.

Finally he made it back to the spot he'd picked out on Mineral Mountain. He sowed the rest of the seeds he'd collected, covering them carefully with soil. Soon they'd start to sprout, and when they opened their beautiful flowers, "WE LOVE SAPPHIRE" would be spelled out on the side of the mountain by the only flowers in Gemstone Valley.

Well, except for the one Opal had, but Emerald put that out of his mind. His gift would be glorious. The Best Gift Ever. Sapphire and all the dragons and magical creatures in Gemstone Valley would see what a great idea he'd had and understand why he'd kept all the seeds from them.

They would. He was sure. He was the one with the gemstone power over plants, anyway. He *should* be the one to have all the flowers for his gift.

Emerald took a deep breath. It had been a long day already, and he still had to find the rest of the lost seeds and put them in his gift before Sapphire got back from the Friendly Forest. He wanted his words to be as full of flowers as possible.

He trudged back down Mineral Mountain.

Then he heard a familiar *RRRRIIIIPPPP* and a shriek.

Oh no, Emerald thought.

The shriek had come from Opal. She was pointing at a green stalk shaking the soil as it emerged from the ground. In no time, it sprouted leaves and then purple flowers.

"It's a flower!" Opal shouted. "A giant flower."

RRIIPPP

"There's another," said Garnet, as another stalk popped out of the ground with a bunch of blue blooms.

"And another!" said Aquamarine,

pointing at another stalk that erupted from the soil covered in red petals.

"Oh no!" Emerald whimpered. "My seeds!"

chapter seven

A GROWING PROBLEM

RRRRIIIPPPP

RRRIIPPPP

RRRRIIIIIIPP

More stalks stretched out of the soil and spread their leaves in the sunlight.

There was no way Emerald could dig them all up and replant them for his Best Gift Ever. Would the gift even be the Best anymore? With fewer flowers, the words wouldn't be as full and pretty. And with giant flowers everywhere, would anyone even care about the ones he'd planted on the side of the mountain?

Worse, Emerald was worried that everyone would find out that he had kept all the seeds for himself without seeing how brilliant the Best Gift Ever could be. If they had seen it the way he'd planned, they would have understood why he had kept it secret. But now . . .

"Emerald, you fixed the flower problem!" Amber said. "How did you do it?"

"I . . . uh . . ." Emerald stared at the ground, hoping he'd find an answer there.

"These are so big. They look like the fake plant you made, Emerald," Aquamarine said. "Are these fake too? I didn't think paper plants grew out of soil."

"These are real, all right," Opal said, smelling a yellow rose the size of her head. "We have plenty of decorations now. Sapphire's birthday party will look beautiful."

"And Sapphire's cake will taste amazing," Diamond said, quickly picking yellow honeysuckle.

"The rest of the food will be wonderful too, now that we have lots of pansies and hibiscus," Topaz said. "I don't know what you did, Emerald, but thank you!"

Emerald's shoulders slumped. Everyone had what they wanted, but his Best Gift Ever was ruined. How was he going to fix it now?

RRRIIIIIPP

RRRIIIPP

RRRRIIIIIIPPP

More stalks tore out of the ground. They were popping up all over Gemstone Valley, in front of fairy hollows and unicorn stables and even next to the gnome huts. Everywhere Emerald looked, his seeds were sprouting giant plants and flowers.

"They're incredible!" Opal said, clapping her paws. Then . . .

CRACK!

The noise was so loud, it took over the air.

"What was that?" Amber asked.

"Our rings!" The shout had come from the unicorn rings. Emerald raced down to see what had happened. Unicorns surrounded the rings they used for their leaping tournaments. The rings lay broken on the ground. Stalks stood tall where the rings had been standing, pushing them out of the way.

"Oh no!" said Opal. She had helped the unicorns put up the largest ring, so she knew how much work it had been.

CRUNCH!

"Ahh," shouted the fairies together. "Our party hollow!"

Emerald and the other dragons dashed to the hollow where the fairies held their parties. Where one of the walls used to be, there was now a giant sunflower, its big face twisting to see the sun. Its stalk had made a hole in the floor, and its leaves were pushing against the windows.

"It's ruined!" said one fairy.

"It's a catastrophe!" said another fairy.

"It's too much flower power," said a third fairy.

CRASH!

This time the sound had come from the Crystal River. Emerald rushed over and saw the latest disaster. A patch of his seeds had sprouted next to one side of the bridge. The plants were so strong, they had pushed through the stones that the bridge was made of. The middle of the bridge had broken, and now the whole thing had collapsed into the water.

Too much flower power indeed.

"Oh no!" said Opal. "This is terrible."

Amber turned to Emerald. "What did you do to fix the flower problem, Emerald?"

"I . . . I didn't do this." Emerald shook his head. He couldn't be responsible for all this. Could he? It was Diamond's tornado that had spread the seeds, but Emerald couldn't tell anyone that, because then they'd know he'd kept them all to himself. And filled them with his gemstone power.

Of course, if he hadn't kept his plan a secret and he'd just told Diamond what he was doing, Diamond wouldn't have made the tornado in the first place.

Emerald tried not to think about that. Flowers—his flowers—were destroying things all over Gemstone Valley.

And he had no idea how to stop them.

"How could this have happened?" Amber stared at Emerald, but he put his paws in the air.

"I don't know. I've never seen plants grow like this before," he said. That was partly true. Until earlier that day, he hadn't.

"Did you use your power to make them grow for Sapphire's party?" Amber asked.

The other dragons and magical creatures had gathered around. They wanted to know how this had happened too. More than anything, they wanted to know how to fix it. And if any creature knew about plants, it was Emerald.

Emerald tried to think of what he could say so they wouldn't be mad at him.

He nodded slowly. "I used a little power to try to make some grow, but nothing like this." He wanted them to think he had been trying to be helpful.

Amber shook her head. "I don't understand what happened."

"How are we going to fix our party hollow?" the fairies said together.

"We're going to have to make new rings," one of the unicorns said.

"What are we going to do about the bridge?" one of the gnomes asked.

Just then, there was a loud *POP*, then a *WHACK*, then a *WHAM*.

"What now?" Amber looked in the direction of the noise and her eyes grew wide. "I hope that's not—"

Amber spread her wings and flew back toward Sparkle Cave.

"What?" Emerald shouted as he followed.

All the dragons and magical creatures ran after Amber, and when they saw what had happened, they let out a loud gasp.

Three plants had burst up under the stage Amber and Obsidian had been building for Sapphire's birthday party. The stalks were so strong, they had ripped the base of the stage and its castle turrets. The throne had been pushed to the ground and splintered into pieces.

Obsidian was standing by the wreckage holding a chunk of the throne. "I couldn't stop it," he said. "They grew so fast."

Emerald looked at Amber. Tears had welled in her eyes.

"Sapphire's birthday party is ruined," Ruby wailed.

chapter eight

A NEW PLAN

A pit grew in Emerald's stomach. He felt terrible. He wanted to tell everyone that he was sorry this had happened, but he didn't want everyone to be mad at him.

His plan had been to make the Best Gift Ever, not the Worst Birthday Ever.

"Sapphire's birthday party won't be ruined," Amber said. "I can use my gemstone power to fix the things that are broken."

"We can all pitch in to help," Opal said.

Emerald nodded enthusiastically. Amber would fix everything. And no one would be mad at him. That made him feel a lot better.

"But we have to stop these plants growing before they break anything else in Gemstone Valley," Amber said. "Emerald, try your power on them."

Emerald's shoulders drooped. He remembered what had happened the last time he'd tried to use his power on one of the plants. "My power only makes the flowers more healthy. It won't stop them from growing."

Amber turned to the fairies. "Maybe some fairy dust would stop them?"

The fairies shook their heads. "Fairy dust only makes things better too," they said in unison.

Amber turned to the unicorns. "Anything you could do?"

"Our magic can't fix this," a unicorn said.

"Ours neither," said one of the gnomes. "These plants are too powerful."

"And they're still growing," Ruby cried, as a poppy shot up next to her. "What are we going to do?"

Amber thought, then said, "We have to cut them down."

"We can't kill them." Opal gasped. "They're so pretty."

A new branch popped out of a hibiscus bush, knocking into Ruby. "Hey," she cried. "Watch where you're growing!"

"Cutting down the plants is the only thing we can do," Amber said. "If we don't get them under control, they'll take over all of Gemstone Valley."

"Amber's right," Obsidian said. "Even beautiful things can be dangerous, especially if there are too many of them."

"We could replant them," Emerald said, an idea forming in his mind.

"Where are we going to put them where they won't cause more damage?" Amber asked.

"Ummm, how about the side of Mineral Mountain?" Emerald didn't tell them he already had the perfect place picked out.

"That's a great idea," Opal said. "As long as they're away from the crystal fields, they shouldn't harm anything there."

Ruby peered up at the mountain as if she were looking for where the flowers could go.

"If we pull the plants up instead of cutting them, we'll preserve the roots," Emerald said.

Aquamarine chuckled. "You mean we could plant them on the *face* of the mountain? You know what kind of flower grows on your face! Tulips. Get it? Like *two lips*." He grabbed the stalk of the tulip next to him and pulled.

Opal giggled. "Here, I'll help you pull it out." They both heaved the stalk, but instead of coming out of the soil, the tulip grew bigger while they were holding onto it. "It won't come up!"

"Stand back," said Obsidian, striding over to the tulip. "This needs my super strength." Obsidian flexed his muscles, then grabbed the stalk and pulled. The flower still wouldn't budge.

"What?" Obsidian frowned. "I didn't think I'd need my gemstone power for some measly plants. This calls for my super *super* strength." His black scales rippled, then the gemstone on his chest glowed. He grabbed the tulip and pulled. And pulled.

And pulled! Finally the soil gave way, and the plant sprang up out of the earth.

"Wow! These plants are extra super strong." Obsidian held up the plant, gazing at its thick roots. "If I can only pull them up using my gemstone power, no one else is going to be able to get them out. But I can't do them all myself before they take over the Valley. I'd also need Garnet's gemstone power of speed for that."

New leaves sprouted on a group of giant daisies next to Emerald, hitting him on the head. He batted at them to keep the leaves back.

"The rest of us can dig them out," he said. "I—" He stopped himself just in time. He had been about to say that he had already dug one out and replanted it successfully, but that would've revealed his secret. "I'm sure that'll work too."

"Another good idea, Emerald," Amber said. "Okay, Obsidian, use your power to pull up as many as you can. Choose the biggest ones, because they'll be hardest for the rest of us."

Obsidian nodded. "I'm on it."

Amber turned to Garnet. "Garnet, can you use your gemstone power of speed to help him get to each plant quickly? They're all over Gemstone Valley."

"I sure can," Garnet said, hopping from paw to paw.

"Excellent. Everyone else can dig," Amber said. "Then, Emerald, you can show us the best place to put them on the mountain."

Emerald smiled. He'd still be able to create the Best Gift Ever. "I'll get some bowls to put the root balls in."

"You mean like this one?" Topaz pointed to the bowl holding the plant Emerald had dug up earlier.

"Yes," Emerald said. "They'll keep the roots safe while we transport the plants."

Topaz looked at the bowl, then at Emerald. "Wait a minute. You said this plant wasn't real and you made the flowers just for Opal and Aquamarine to use for decorations."

Emerald didn't like where this was going. "Uh huh."

"But if it's not one of these big plants,

why does it need to be in a bowl?"

"Ummm. I thought it looked pretty?" Emerald didn't like where this was going at all.

Ruby had been staring at Mineral Mountain. "Is it me, or does it look like there's a word on the side of the mountain?"

Emerald turned to look, along with everyone else. The seeds he had planted for Sapphire's gift must have sprouted, and now the letters *WE LO   SAP* could be seen in bright colors.

Amber peered at it. "Those look like they're made out of flowers. Big flowers like the ones on all these plants." She swung back around to face Emerald. "Emerald?"

Emerald's face suddenly felt hot. All the dragons and magical creatures were

staring at him. And they didn't look happy. Emerald was stuck. He didn't want to admit how badly he'd messed up. He didn't want the other dragons to be mad at him. But he couldn't lie to them. Not now.

"I did it," he cried. "I've been storing up seeds for months. That's why there weren't many flowers growing. Then I put all my gemstone power into the seeds and I started to plant them on the side of Mineral Mountain. I was going to make the Best Gift Ever for Sapphire. It would say *WE LOVE SAPPHIRE* in big flowers, so it could be seen from all over Gemstone Valley. And it worked. Look!" He pointed to the letters visible on the side of Mineral Mountain.

"But Diamond's tornado spread the

seeds everywhere. I tried to find them, but they started to grow. I dug up the first one and was going to replant it on the mountain, but when Opal saw the flower, I said it was fake so no one would find out the truth."

He turned to the unicorns. "I'm really sorry about your rings. And your party room, fairies. And the bridge. And Amber and Obsidian, I'm so sorry about the stage you built. It was wonderful. I didn't mean for any of this to happen."

"So you kept all the flowers for yourself?" Opal stared at Emerald.

"And you lied when we said we needed flowers?" Amber shook her head.

"And now you want to replant the

flowers so you can still make your gift?" Ruby crossed her arms tightly.

"I just . . . I . . ." Emerald gazed at all the other dragons, and they all glared back at him. "I'm sorry." Then Emerald spread his wings and quickly flew away.

chapter nine

THE BEST THING ABOUT FLOWERS

Emerald flew over to the broken bridge at the Crystal River. He felt like his heart was in his tail. He had wanted to make Sapphire's birthday the best it could be and to have all the dragons and creatures be proud of him. Instead, he had made this the worst party ever. All the dragons should've been making final preparations now, but they were all working hard to fix the destruction his giant flowers had caused.

Worst of all, everyone was mad at him. And he didn't know how to fix that.

As he dug at the soil around one of the plants, he heard a gasp behind him. He turned to find Sapphire flying over the river. She landed next to him, staring at the smashed bridge.

"Sapphire!" Emerald stood up quickly. He had hoped everything would be fixed before she saw what had happened.

"It looks like there's been quite an adventure here while I've been visiting the Friendly Forest. But what a lovely flower this is." Sapphire sniffed the large white gardenia and smiled.

"Don't worry, Sapphire. Amber is going to fix the bridge."

"Oh, I have no doubt about that." Sapphire grinned. "The Gemstone Dragons are very resourceful and always do what's right, don't you think?"

Emerald hung his head. "Not always," he muttered.

"Is something bothering you, Emerald?"

Emerald didn't want to spoil Sapphire's birthday party surprise, but he could really use her wisdom right now. He didn't know how to make things right with the other dragons and magical creatures.

"It's just . . ." He thought of the best way to say it. "I have this friend, and they had a whole lot of mangoes but they kept them all to themself. They hid the mangoes so no one else could have one, and they planned to make a really good mango pie, like the best mango pie ever. They thought everyone would love that."

Emerald glanced up at Sapphire to see if she looked mad, but the blue dragon gazed back at him. *"Mm hmm."*

"Well," Emerald continued, "something happened, and the mangoes messed up all the food in the kitchen before my friend could make their pie. So then, no one could have the mangoes, and all the other food was messed up too. Everyone was really mad at my friend for keeping all the mangoes. And they never even got to have the best mango pie that my friend had planned to make."

Emerald's snout drooped. He waited to
hear Sapphire's response. When she didn't
immediately say anything, he glanced up
and saw that she was smiling sadly.

"I think the worst part is that my friend was being selfish," Emerald said, after thinking a bit more. "They didn't want to make the best mango pie so everyone else would enjoy it. Really, deep down, they wanted to do it so everyone would be proud of them and think they were the best drag—I mean, *friend* of all. They wanted everyone else to tell them they were good. And that's why they kept all the mangoes."

Emerald sighed. He didn't need Sapphire to tell him he—or his "friend"— had done the wrong thing. He knew it now right down to the tip of his tail. "My friend should've shared the mangoes. Then they could've had mango pie, and mango cake, and mango cookies." He nodded to himself, thinking about how great his Best Gift

Ever could've been if he had trusted the other dragons to help him with it instead of keeping it all to himself. "Yeah, that really would've been the best, because they could've all made things together. Don't you think?"

He waited for Sapphire to say something. He hoped she'd say that the creature would be forgiven and the others wouldn't be mad at them for long.

"Your friend has a good heart. It's easy for hearts to be in the wrong place sometimes, even with the best of intentions." Sapphire patted him on the shoulder. "It reminds me of a time when I was a younger dragon. I had made some wonderful potassium toffee. I love potassium toffee. It's one of my favorite treats. But we didn't have a good crop of potassium that year, and I couldn't make very much. I desperately wanted to keep all the potassium toffee for myself."

"What did you do?" Emerald asked.

"I hid it away in my bedcave, so that no one would know I had it and I wouldn't have to share it. Then I ate and ate. I ate half of it all by myself."

Sapphire cleared her throat, as though the memory was difficult to get out.

"But after a while, I realized that all my friends were outside playing and I was all alone. That wasn't fun at all. So I decided to share the last half of the potassium toffee. And do you know what I discovered?"

Emerald shook his head. He couldn't imagine, but he really wanted to know.

Sapphire leaned in closer, as though she were going to tell Emerald a secret.

"I discovered something even better than potassium toffee—my friends' smiles." She beamed at Emerald as though showing him how wonderful a smile could be. "I think that one of the best gifts we can ever get is a smile from some other creature. Don't you?"

Emerald nodded enthusiastically. He loved smiles.

Then his heart dropped, as he remembered that all the creatures in Gemstone Valley were mad at him and wouldn't be smiling at him for a while. If they ever did again.

"Like these flowers," Sapphire continued, staring at the gardenia bush.

"They are absolutely beautiful. But do you know what I like best about flowers?"

Emerald's eyes grew bigger with Sapphire's mention of the flowers. She couldn't have known what he'd done, could she?

"What I like best about flowers," Sapphire said, "is how they make everyone around me smile."

She sniffed the gardenia again. "And they smell nice too." She grinned.

"Now," Sapphire continued, "I just remembered something else I have to do in the Friendly Forest. I'm afraid it's going to be a bit longer before I can get back to Shimmering Hall. I do hope you'll let everyone know. I'm looking forward to seeing them when I return."

"Of course," Emerald said, grateful that they still had time to prepare for her party.

Sapphire lifted her dark blue wings and flew back toward the Friendly Forest.

As Emerald watched her go, he thought about her words.

It wasn't just the flowers that Sapphire loved. What she loved best was the joy that flowers brought everyone around her. Sapphire's best present was seeing all the other dragons and magical creatures happy.

But today, on her birthday, Emerald had taken all the joy out of Gemstone Valley.

He had to find a way to get it back.

And he was starting to get an idea . . .

chapter ten

THE BEST GIFT EVER

· ⁎ ⁎ ⁎ ⁎ ⁎ ⁎ ⁎ ⁎

Emerald quickly finished digging up the giant flower bushes that had broken the bridge. Then he dragged them to where Amber and Obsidian had been setting up the stage for Sapphire's birthday.

Lots of other dragons and magical creatures were also there, standing around the stage. Amber had used her gemstone power of fixing things, and the stage now stood tall, with all its turrets and the throne back in place, as though nothing had happened. Emerald couldn't see any of the giant flowers, so he guessed they must've all been destroyed so they wouldn't cause any more damage.

"Emerald!" Amber said when she saw him.

"The stage looks fantastic," Emerald said shyly.

"Thank you. It took a lot of gemstone power to fix the unicorn rings, the fairy house, and this, and I still have to do the bridge." She sighed. "It will be done soon, though. Are those the plants from the river?"

Emerald nodded.

"Good," Amber said. "Look, Emerald, I want to say something to you."

Emerald could just imagine what Amber was going to say. How he had been selfish and uncaring, how he'd messed up Sapphire's birthday, how none of the dragons or magical creatures wanted to talk to him ever again.

He couldn't let that happen.

"I've got something to say to you too," he said quickly. "In fact, I've got something I want to say to everyone."

Emerald climbed onto the stage and looked out at all his friends. The dragons, unicorns, and all the other magical creatures stared up at him. Emerald felt his tummy turn over with nerves. But he had to stay strong. He had to tell them everything.

He took a deep breath, then began.

"I want you all to know that I'm very sorry for everything that happened. When I started keeping the seeds, I only kept a few. But then I saw more seeds, and I thought I'd need them too. The more seeds I kept for myself, the more I wanted to have every single one."

Emerald swallowed. All the dragons and magical creatures were watching him. He hoped they would forgive him.

"Everyone always does great things for Sapphire's birthday, and I wanted to make her something she really loved. I thought that if I had all the seeds, I could do that. But the real truth is that I wanted my gift to be better than anyone else's."

The dragons and magical creatures started to murmur to each other, and

Emerald worried that they would be even more mad at him.

"But I realize now that even if my plan had worked perfectly, my gift would never have been the Best Gift Ever," he continued.

Everyone looked at Emerald, confused.

"The Best Gift Ever is one you share with everyone," he said. "I know we can't do my original gift anymore, but if you'll let me, I think I can make it up to you."

Amber walked up to him. Emerald hoped telling her this hadn't made her even more mad. He held his breath.

But Amber looked at him kindly. "Emerald, you don't have anything to make up to us. You left before we could say anything. We were disappointed you hadn't trusted us with your secret because if you had told us, we would've helped you with the flower sign. Wouldn't we?"

Amber looked out at the crowd of magical creatures.

"Yes," said Opal.

"That's right," said Obsidian.

"We love the idea," said the fairies in unison.

"Yeah," said Amber. "We all love Sapphire, and the flower garden is a wonderful way to let her know."

"You really think so?" Emerald said, his heart bursting with joy. Then he got sad again. "I wish I had finished it. In fact, I wish we had all done it together."

"Well, we sort of did." Amber grinned, then pointed toward Mineral Mountain.

From where he was standing, Emerald

could see *WE LOVE SAPPHIRE* glowing in beautiful flowery colors from the side of the mountain.

"But how? All the flowers were destroyed." Emerald couldn't stop staring at the wonderful words.

"Not exactly," Opal said, stepping up. "We couldn't let a good idea go to waste, so as soon as we dug up a plant, Garnet flew it up there and got it planted. I don't know if they're in the order you wanted."

"They're perfect," Emerald said, smiling. Then he remembered Sapphire's words. "But for Sapphire's birthday party, I actually have another idea that I think she'll like even better."

Everyone leaned in close to hear.

It didn't take long for the dragons to

do Emerald's plan. By the time Sapphire arrived back at Sparkle Cave, everything was ready for her birthday party.

Diamond's cake was decorated with yellow carnations and had lots of honeysuckle nectar inside, just the way Sapphire liked it.

Ruby and Topaz had put Sapphire's favorite edible flowers into all her favorite foods too. They'd made creamy cadmium quiche with daylilies, magnesium noodle salad with black locust flowers, and zinc-crusted mushroom caps topped with mustard flowers. They'd also made pitchers of mimosa flower cordial, and Emerald had asked them to add another dessert to the menu: potassium toffee.

Opal and Aquamarine had decorated the

grounds with pink roses, white lilies, and purple pansies. The stage was covered in blooms, with poppies and hibiscus all over the turrets, and jasmine and geraniums around the throne.

As a final touch, the unicorns had sent rainbow-colored sparkles from their horns to spread out on top of everything.

"My, my," Sapphire exclaimed as she landed. "This looks spectacular!"

"Happy Birthday!" all the dragons and magical creatures cried out together.

Sapphire beamed. "What a wonderful surprise. I have no idea how you did all this so quickly."

"We've got a fun party planned for you, Sapphire," Amber said. "Actually, it'll be a fun party for all of us."

She looked at Emerald and smiled. He felt warm all over.

"Emerald," Amber said, "tell Sapphire what we've done."

"Me?" Emerald didn't think he deserved to be the one to show Sapphire everything, especially since his first plan had almost ruined her party.

"Yes. It was your idea!" said Amber.

"Go on," said Opal.

"Show her! Show her!" said Ruby.

Sapphire walked up to Emerald. "I would love to hear what you have in store."

Emerald smiled at Sapphire and all his friends. "Well, we're going to have a great party. For all of us." Emerald started walking Sapphire around. "We've got painting with flower paints, making daisy chains, and

Pin the Petal on the Sunflower. There's an apple dunk in rosewater. And Pearl is making ice sculptures, and everyone can guess which flowers they are."

"So many flowery games," Sapphire said, looking around. "It's absolutely flower-tastic." She clapped her paws.

"We all did it together," Emerald said. He glanced at the other dragons and magical creatures. They were all smiling, just like Sapphire had wanted.

Emerald smiled too. He realized he had done what he wanted to after all. This really was Sapphire's Best Gift Ever.

SOME FACTS ABOUT EMERALDS!

COLOR: Emeralds are a vibrant green color and have tiny fractures inside that are known as the "jardin," the Spanish word for garden.

BIRTHSTONE: The emerald is the birthstone for people born in May.

MEANING: Emeralds are thought to promote love and friendship, keeping partnerships in balance. A long time ago, some people also believed that emeralds could help you tell the future!

FUN FACTS: When they're found in the ground, emeralds look like six-sided crystals grouped together. The oldest emeralds were found in South Africa and are about three billion years old!

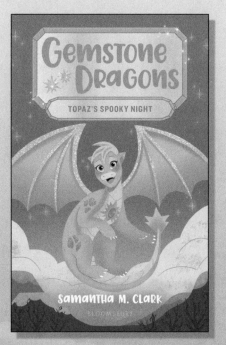

It was a beautiful clear night in Gemstone Valley with only a sliver of moon in the sky. The dragons were on top of Mineral Mountain enjoying a meteor shower. The dark night made the stars look extra bright, but it also made Topaz extra nervous.

Topaz didn't like the dark. When she couldn't see, she was afraid monsters were going to jump out at her.

She concentrated on the topaz gemstone on her chest, activating its power, and as her yellow-brown scales rippled, light glowed all around her. She felt much better.

"Why are you turning on your light out here, Topaz?" Emerald asked.

"I don't want anyone to trip on a rock," Topaz said, which was only a little true. She didn't want to admit the real reason.

"That's very nice of you," Ruby said. Topaz loved the way her best friend always defended her.

"Thank you, Ruby." Topaz gave her a small smile.

"It is nice, but then we can't see the stars," Emerald said. "You can turn it off now. We'll be all right."

"That reminds me of a joke." Aquamarine

did a little skip. "Why did the monster eat Topaz? Because it wanted a light lunch! Get it? Because her power is light?" He bent over laughing, but the other dragons didn't find it funny, especially Topaz. She didn't want to think about being eaten by a monster.

Aquamarine gazed at the dragons' stern faces. "Okay, okay. How about this one: What happens when Topaz uses her light too much? She gets burned out! Get it? Like a torch burns out." He laughed again, and this time some of the other dragons laughed too.

"Aquamarine, you say the silliest jokes," Emerald said. "That gives me a great idea. After Topaz has turned out her light, let's start a bonfire and tell scary stories in the dark!"

"Yes!" Ruby jumped up and down. "I love scary stories."

"Me too," said Aquamarine. "Do you know what a ghost's favorite food is? Ice scream! Get it? Like ice cream."

Ruby and Emerald laughed harder this time. Topaz had to admit that this joke was pretty funny, but she could only laugh a little. She did not like the idea of sitting in the dark telling scary stories at all. The darkness was scary enough! She didn't need scary stories to make it worse.

But she didn't want the other dragons to know she was afraid. What would they think of her then?

"We could go back to Sparkle Cave and tell stories there," Topaz said. Even at night, Sparkle Cave was lit up with torches. She wouldn't be scared telling stories there, and even if she was, she could pretend to be tired and go back to her bedcave. She liked this idea much better.

"It'll be more fun out here in the dark with a fire," Emerald said. He settled on the ground and motioned for Ruby, Aquamarine, and Topaz to sit down too. Telling scary stories was a sitting kind of activity.

Topaz glanced at the path to Sparkle Cave. She could make an excuse and go home, like say she was tired or hungry. Then she could leave the darkness and the scary stories behind and no one would know she was scared.

But she didn't like walking around Gemstone Valley by herself when it was

dark. Even if she turned her gemstone light on, it would only light up the path, and the darkness beyond could still be filled with monsters. She knew all too well how scary the darkness could be. One time she had been caught in the Friendly Forest during a blizzard in the dark, and that had been very scary indeed.

If Ruby went with her, Topaz wouldn't be as scared. Topaz was sure Ruby would go if she asked. But Ruby was already sprawled out on the ground next to Emerald and Aquamarine, excited to hear the stories. She had even used her gemstone power over fire to balance a fireball between them. Ruby was so brave. Topaz didn't want Ruby to know she was scared.

There was no other choice. Topaz had to turn off her light and stay.

"Okay," she said, as her light slowly went away. "This is going to be fun." But she didn't believe that for one second.

Aquamarine told a story first, and luckily, it wasn't too scary. Topaz actually thought it was pretty funny. It was about a bunny with fangs, but the only things it killed were carrots. Listening to the story, Topaz forgot all about the dark. She laughed along with Emerald and Ruby.

Next, Ruby told a story about a skeleton that grew out of the ground. That sounded very scary to Topaz! But Ruby's skeleton just liked to dance. Topaz was relieved.

When Ruby finished, Emerald gave

them a toothy grin. "I've got a good story for you." He leaned closer to the fireball, so the flames sent shadows over his face. He looked scary. Topaz leaned farther away.

SAMANTHA M. CLARK is a storyteller, a daydreamer, and the author of a number of books for young readers. Most of the time, she lives in her head with a magical tree, a forest of talking animals, and a sky filled with pink fluffy clouds. Like the Gemstone Dragons, she knows the best power in the world is friendship.

HOLLIE HIBBERT is an illustrator. Like these dragons, Hollie treasures friendships. Her friends help her face scary spiders and remind her to charge her phone. When she isn't drawing or painting, she loves to travel, play the piano, and collect shiny things.

JANELLE ANDERSON is an illustrator who is happiest when bringing the images in her head to life. Some of her favorite things to draw are colorful mountains, sparkly waterfalls, and magical creatures just like the Gemstone Dragons. She loves the outdoors and making people smile, and believes there is a little bit of magic in everyone.